The Adventures of Everyday Geniuses

Mrs. Gorski, I Think I Have the Wiggle Fidgets

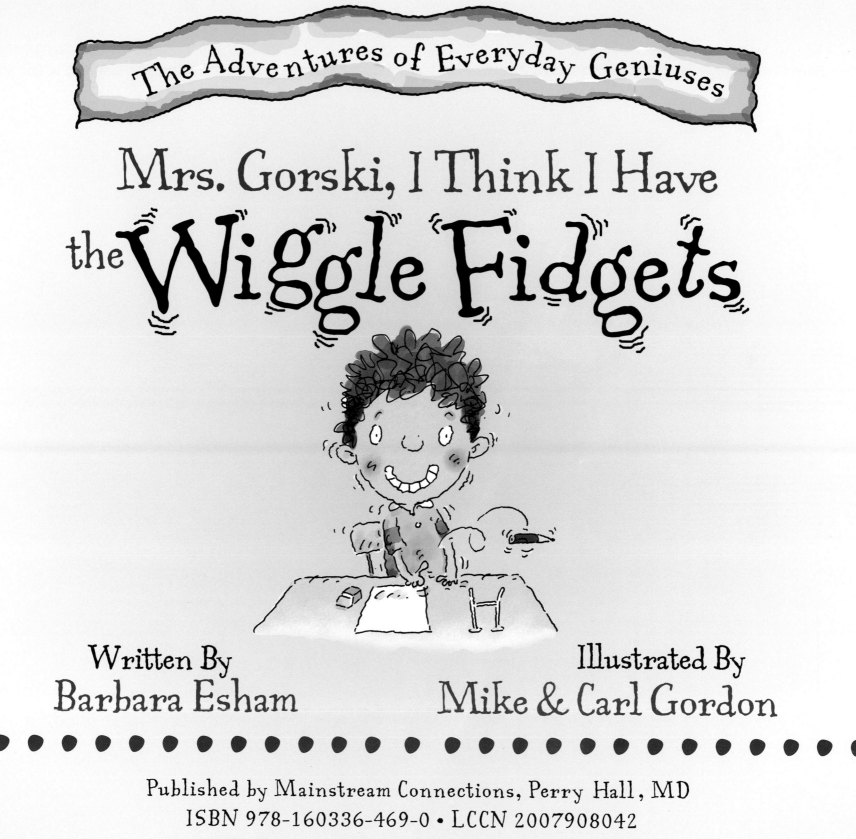

Written By
Barbara Esham

Illustrated By
Mike & Carl Gordon

Published by Mainstream Connections, Perry Hall, MD
ISBN 978-160336-469-0 • LCCN 2007908042

"David Sheldon, you are distracting your neighbor again," said Mrs. Gorski with her serious voice. "You are going to have to stop making that noise with your pencil!"

I tried to explain that I only wanted to see how many times I could roll my pencil to the very edge of my desk without it falling off, but Mrs. Gorski interrupted me.

"I do not need an explanation, David, but I do need you to pay attention in class."

1

Once again, everyone in the class was staring at me.
I get the feeling Mrs. Gorski doesn't like me very much.
I can tell by the way her voice changes when she speaks to me.
It's her "Speaking to David" voice.

I know that I bug her;
I just don't know how to stop.

The problem is, I'm not thinking about paying attention when I'm not paying attention. If I was thinking about paying attention when I'm not paying attention, I would definitely pay attention. I want to pay attention but it is just so hard when an exciting idea pops into my head. Nothing else seems important when there are ideas to think about.

Every day I do something that upsets Mrs. Gorski. I never mean to do it, but it happens anyway. Like the time we had our first fire drill. I really made her mad that day...

Mrs. Gorski told us to stand single file, on the line, in the parking lot. I really tried to pay attention and follow the instructions, but I got a really good idea...

I wanted to see
how long
I could stand
on one foot...
with my eyes closed...
with both hands
on my shoulders...
while hopping in place...
while standing
single file,
on the line,
in the parking lot.

4

I was following Mrs. Gorski's directions,
except I was on one foot... until I fell down.

Maybe she got upset because our class was the only one
that wasn't standing during the fire drill.

But that was nothing compared to yesterday in the cafeteria.
It all started with a pudding cup — and an idea...

I wasn't trying to make a mess. I just wanted to see how much
pressure the lid could take before...
well, you can imagine.

6

I didn't see Mrs. Gorski standing behind me, and
I didn't think a pudding cup could make such a mess.

"What possesses you to do such things, David?" Mrs. Gorski
asked with her angry "Speaking to David" voice.

I tried to explain I didn't think
the pudding would shoot that far,
but she interrupted me.

"David, I will be sending a note
home to your parents."

I don't know why I do what I do!

I can always see the mistakes I make – after I make them.
But before they're mistakes, they just seem like great ideas.

I wish I could stop myself.
I wish I would think a little more before I test my great ideas.

I wish I didn't get on everyone's nerves.

That night I listened while my parents talked about Mrs. Gorski's letter.

"David just has the wiggle fidgets. I had the wiggle fidgets when I was a kid. I had so many ideas bouncing around in my mind that it was impossible for me to sit still," my dad told my mom.

"Mrs. Gorski wants to meet with us Monday afternoon," my mom replied.

10

I have until Monday to think of a plan, and I know what I have to do. I'll have to find a cure for the wiggle fidgets!

I know I'm not the only kid who suffers from the wiggle fidgets.

This could be my greatest discovery yet!

I spent most of Saturday afternoon brainstorming.
I'm great at that.
Brainstorming is one of my strengths.

I have to be careful that none of my cures for the wiggle fidgets are distracting to me or my class or Mrs. Gorski.

In other words, I have to think about consequences. I hope my parents and Mrs. Gorski will be proud of me for a change.

Monday after school I went to my locker to get what I needed for the meeting: my notebook and my...

box of cures.

I found my parents and Mrs. Gorski in the classroom.

Using my most serious voice, I said,
"Mom, Dad, Mrs. Gorski, on Saturday I discovered exactly
what my problem is. I learned some important information
that has inspired me to come up with a cure for this
very serious — but common — problem."

I looked at my dad before I said, "The problem I have is called
the wiggle fidgets!
It is something that you can inherit from your parents,
or you can just have it. I inherited it from my dad.
The difference is I have come up with a cure.
It took all day on Saturday to develop it."

16

My parents and Mrs. Gorski just listened.

"I have come up with a few things that will help me pay attention better," I announced while spreading some note cards on the table. "These are my attention cards--patent pending."

"If I put one of these cards on my desk, it will remind me to focus and leave the distracting ideas and thoughts alone."

"This way, Mrs. Gorski, you can save your voice and I can save myself from becoming embarrassed. Everyone in the class becomes distracted when you tell me to pay attention."

FOCUS and LISTEN

ATTENTION!

THINK about what we are WORKING ON!

What are the CONSEQUENCES?

"But that's not my only cure for the wiggle fidgets. I also have a timer that ticks silently. I've discovered that, if I know exactly how long I need to pay attention, it keeps me from wondering about how long I need to pay attention."

I couldn't believe it; Mrs. Gorski was actually **smiling at me!** She hasn't smiled at me for a long, long, long time.

I have a feeling she likes my cures.

19

Then, using my serious announcement voice, I said,
"For the super wiggly fidget days,
I need to have something to do. Even if it is just a
small something to fidget with, like this stress ball.

I've noticed that when I fidget with the stress ball at home,
it actually helps me pay attention. I'm not sure exactly
how it works, but I know it does."

I hoped Mrs. Gorski
was still listening.

"Another way to make the wiggle fidgets go away is to move just a little. Sometimes my legs feel like they are going to run away without me. If I could just erase the chalkboard or hand out papers or, better yet, run your papers to the office, my legs might not be so wiggly at my desk."

I wanted to help Mrs. Gorski understand.

"Well, that's all I have for today. I will be available to answer questions if anyone has them," I said as I collected my items.

"David, I am quite impressed," Mrs. Gorski announced in a voice that wasn't angry. "I think your ideas are wonderful. We will start using them tomorrow. Of course we will have to keep your cures from becoming a distraction for the rest of the class, but I am sure we can make this work."

"Your cures might work well at home too," said my mom.

"David, you always come up with the most original ideas.
You remind me of a kid that I used to know,"
my dad added with a smile and a wink.

"You know, Mrs. Gorski, I was thinking," I said, feeling quite confident. "I think my box of cures might help Jeremy too. He doesn't move around as much as I do, but I can tell that he gets tired of sitting sometimes, especially during social studies. I also notice that Karina becomes distracted by Timmy when he acts silly. Timmy is quiet, but he can sure round up an audience when he does his clown-nose routine! Maybe some of the other kids in our class will wiggle and fidget less with a little help."

24

"I think your plan is going to help me manage the entire classroom's wiggle fidgets," Mrs. Gorski replied with a smile.

"I can remember when I had the wiggle fidgets. I couldn't wait to get up from my desk during science class to touch the project materials or look through the microscope. I can remember Mrs. Smith, my science teacher, telling me to sit still or I wouldn't get to do the science activity."

"Mrs. Gorski,
you had the wiggle fidgets too?"

"David, many great minds come with the wiggle fidgets," she answered with a smile. I noticed she wasn't using her angry "Speaking with David" voice anymore.

From Dr. Edward Hallowell,

New York Times national best seller, former Harvard Medical School instructor, and current director of the Hallowell Center for Cognitive and Emotional Health...

Fear is the great disabler. Fear is what keeps children from realizing their potential. It needs to be replaced with a feeling of I-know-I-can-make-progress-if-I-keep-trying-and-boy-do-I-ever-want-to-do-that!

One of the great goals of parents, teachers, and coaches should be to find areas in which a child might experience mastery, then make it possible for the child to feel this potent sensation.

The feeling of mastery transforms a child from a reluctant, fearful learner into a self-motivated player.

The mistake that parents, teachers, and coaches often make is that they demand mastery rather than lead children to it by helping them overcome the fear of failure.

The best parents are great teachers. My definition of a great teacher is a person who can lead another person to mastery.

~Dr. Hallowell

To read Dr. Hallowell's full letter, go to our website! Check out what ALL THE OTHER EXPERTS are saying about The Adventures of Everyday Geniuses book series. www.MainstreamConnections.org

A Note to Parents & Teachers

Mainstream Connections would like to help you help your kids become **Everyday Geniuses!**

These fun stories are an easy way to discuss learning styles and obstacles that can impede a child's potential.

The science of learning is making its way into the classroom! Everyday Geniuses are making their debut!

Call, email, or visit the website to learn how YOU can make a difference.

All books are available in bulk at discount for qualifying schools and professional organizations. Contact us!

RESOURCES for PARENTS and TEACHERS

The BIG LIST of resources can be found on our **website**. The big list is for parents and teachers, you know, just to give them the latest information on how our brains really learn, and what **being smart** is all about.

The topic of this book – Attention – is a complex topic, one which needs to be explored by professionals, and understood by parents and educators. Many experts define "Attention" not as a single function, but the end result of many functions that need to work together.

Mainstream Connections provides **you** respected **resources** to help you create a happy, healthy learning environment for every child.

DOWNLOAD your complimentary Resource List today!

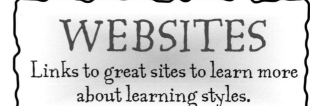

WEBSITES
Links to great sites to learn more about learning styles.

BOOK LISTS
Learn what the experts say about learning styles and obstacles.

CONNECT
News, info & support!

www.MainstreamConnections.org

The Mainstream Connections mission is to expose the broader definitions of learning, creativity, and intelligence. A substantial portion of all profits is held to fund and support the development of programs and services to give all children the tools needed for success.

Are you an EVERYDAY GENIUS TOO?

Get online with your favorite characters from

The Adventures of Everyday Geniuses

There is SO MUCH to do online!

- Meet the Gang and see what they are up to: ideas, inventions and algorithms, poems and other literary works, Eduardo's latest recipe, and get a list of great minds from the past and present!
- Download pages for coloring!
- Hats, Shirts, Classroom Stuff!

www.MainstreamConnections.org

Visit our website to learn more! Adults should always supervise children's web activity.

BOOK INFORMATION

Mrs. Gorski, I Think I Have the Wiggle Fidgets
written by Barbara Esham illustrated by Mike & Carl Gordon

Published by Mainstream Connections Publishing
P.O. Box 398, Perry Hall Maryland 21128

Copyright © 2008, Barbara Esham. All rights reserved.

No part of this publication may be reproduced in whole or in part, in any form without permission from the publisher. *The Adventures of Everyday Geniuses* is a registered trademark.

Book design by Pneuma Books, LLC. www.pneumabooks.com
Printed in China ∞ Library Binding

FIRST EDITION

15 14 13 12 11 10 09 08   01 02 03 04 05 06 07 08

CATALOGING-IN-PUBLICATION DATA

Esham, Barbara.

Mrs. Gorski, I think I have the wiggle fidgets / written by Barbara Esham ; illustrated by Mike & Carl Gordon. -- 1st ed. -- Perry Hall, MD : Mainstream Connections, 2008.

p. ; cm.

(Adventures of everyday geniuses)

ISBN: 978-1-60336-469-0

Audience: Ages 5-10.

Summary: David Sheldon finds it difficult to pay attention and follow directions. His teacher, Mrs. Gorski, has had enough of David's brainstorms, but David "brainstorms" a way to manage his "wiggle fidgets".

1. Attention-deficit-disordered children--Juvenile fiction. 2. Hyperactive children--Juvenile fiction. 3. Self-esteem--Juvenile fiction. 4. Anxiety--Juvenile fiction. 5. Learning disabled children--Juvenile fiction. 6. Cognitive styles in children. 7. [Attention-deficit hyperactivity disorder--Fiction. 8. Anxiety--Fiction. 9. Learning disabilities--Fiction.] I. Gordon, Mike. II. Gordon, Carl. III. Title. IV. Series.

PZ7.E74583 M77 2008   2007908042

[Fic] dc22   0803